J
PIC
HAR

Harper, Charise
  Mericle.

Henry's heart.

DATE		

If you have a home computer with internet access you may:
  -request an item be placed on hold
  -renew an item that is overdue
  -view titles and due dates checked out on your card
  -view your own outstanding fines

To view your patron record from your home computer:
Click on the NSPL homepage:
http://nspl.suffolk.lib.ny.us

HENRY'S DAD

I love Henry's energy.

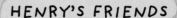

HENRY'S FRIENDS

We love playing with Henry.

This book belongs to

I ♥

I love Henry's smile.

HENRY'S MOM

I love my new shoes. Henry better not touch them.

HENRY'S SISTER

Henry's Heart

A Boy, His Heart, and a New Best Friend

by Charise Mericle Harper

Christy Ottaviano Books

Henry Holt and Company • New York

Her heart
is beating
with love.

This book is
dedicated to all
the students of
Daniel Warren
Elementary School.

CHRISTY, MY
LOVELY EDITOR

I'm all
about
healthy
eating.

Henry Holt and Company, LLC
Publishers since 1866
175 Fifth Avenue
New York, New York 10010
mackids.com

Henry Holt® is a registered trademark of
Henry Holt and Company, LLC.
Copyright © 2011 by Charise Mericle Harper
All rights reserved.

Library of Congress Cataloging-in-Publication Data
Harper, Charise Mericle.
Henry's heart / by Charise Mericle Harper. — 1st ed.
p.   cm.
"Christy Ottaviano Books."
Summary: When Henry falls in love with a puppy but his
father will not buy it for him, his heart reacts strangely.
Includes facts about the heart's role within the body.
ISBN 978-0-8050-8989-9 (hc)
[1. Heart—Fiction. 2. Family life—Fiction.] I. Title.
PZ7.H231323He 2011 [E]—dc22   2010040321

First Edition—2011 / Designed by Elynn Cohen
Acrylic paint and collage on watercolor paper
were used to create the illustrations for this book.
Medical illustrations are not actual size and, please
remember, they are only approximations.
Printed in August 2011 in China by Macmillan
Production Asia Ltd., Kwun Tong, Kowloon,
Hong Kong (supplier code: WKT)

10 9 8 7 6 5 4 3 2 1

KINDERGARTEN

Mrs. Blaney
Ryan
Devin
Nathan
Angela
Emelin
Sebastian
Olivia
Joseph
Hank

Samantha
Luke
Chantal
Peter
Cole
Kiera
Reiko
Julia
Alice
Olivis
Jason

Ms. D'Alesandro
Bella
Madison
Benjamin
Daniel
Chase
Alana
Kyle

Zachary
Cole
Luther
Sophie
Emma
Lily
James
Evelyn
Asher
Regan
Jessica
Ava
Timothy
Kaitlyn

Ms. Lewis
Abigail
Alessandra
Zachary
Marianna
Kymberly
Momo
Scott
Isaac
Neri
Erin
Shudai
Abby

Here is Henry's body. If you had
X-ray vision, this is some of
what you might see:

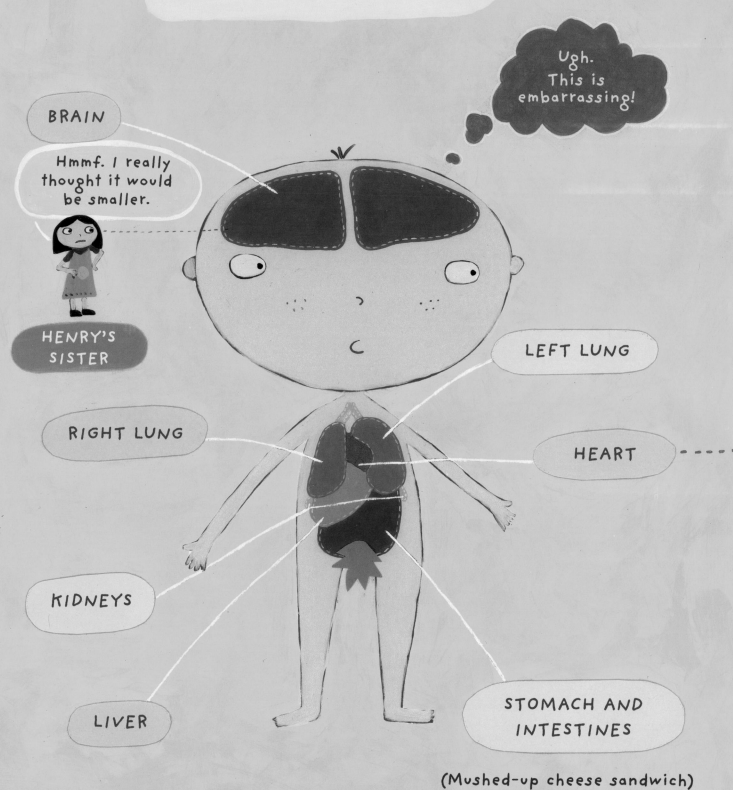

(Mushed-up cheese sandwich)

Many people think hearts look like this:

I'm all about hearts.

That heart is so cute.

But a real heart looks more like this (without the eyes and mouth, of course):

This is a close-up of Henry's heart.

Ewww! What is that thing?

It's a model of my heart. I made it for you.

Excuse me, but you're wearing your heart on your sleeve.

Oops.

If you had X-ray vision,
this is some of what you might see:

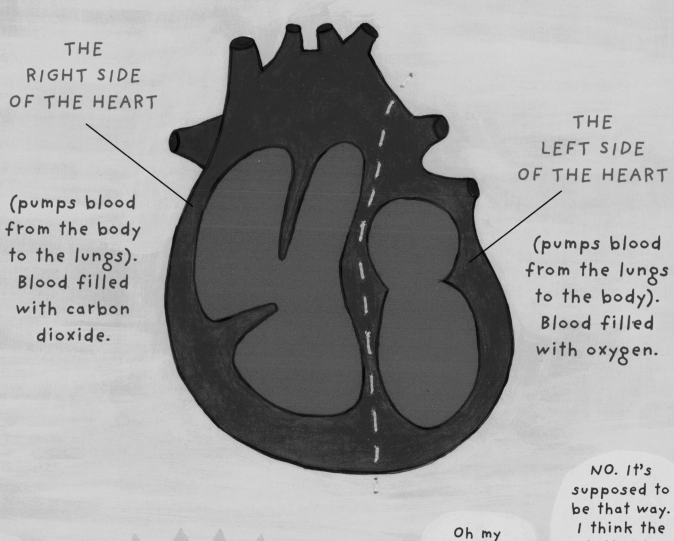

THE
RIGHT SIDE
OF THE HEART

(pumps blood
from the body
to the lungs).
Blood filled
with carbon
dioxide.

THE
LEFT SIDE
OF THE HEART

(pumps blood
from the lungs
to the body).
Blood filled
with oxygen.

One of the most
surprising things
about the heart is
that it actually
has two parts.

Oh my
gosh. Is it
broken?

NO. It's
supposed to
be that way.
I think the
left side
is cuter.

FIRST AID

Both sides of the heart work together to pump blood to and from all parts of the body.

Blood delivers food AND takes away waste.

Henry's heart is very chatty. Here is what he has to say about himself:

I'm about the same size as Henry's fist.

I'm mostly muscle.

I think of myself as a pump— without me the blood can't move. I send blood through Henry's whole body. Every heartbeat pushes the blood farther and farther. This is called circulation.

When Henry is resting and not moving around, I beat between 80 and 100 beats a minute.

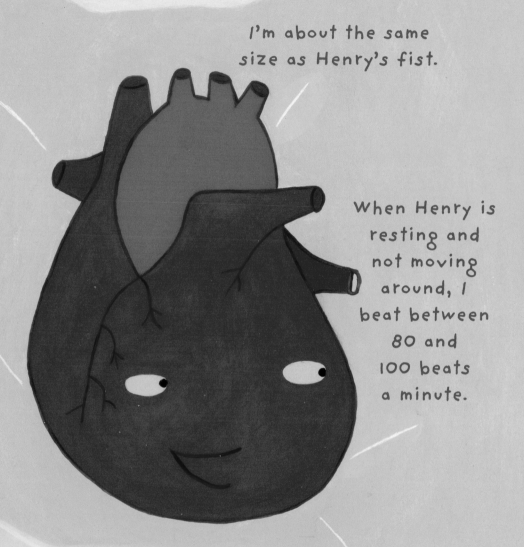

I work every minute of every day and night. I'm on the job 24/7 because a heart can't take a vacation from circulation!

I'm mostly muscle too!

No you're not. Those are balloons.

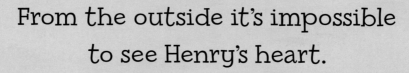
From the outside it's impossible to see Henry's heart.

Henry's heart works perfectly. Henry can do jumping jacks, handstands, and even play video games without ever thinking about what his heart is doing. Henry's mother is not like Henry. She thinks about Henry's heart.

ON SUNNY DAYS, HENRY'S MOTHER LIKES HENRY AND HIS HEART TO GET SOME EXERCISE.

HENRY MALCOLM WEBBER, you should be outside playing in the fresh air.

FIFTY-ONE

If your mom uses your whole, entire name in a sentence, then you should listen to her and do what she says, or you might get in big trouble.

It happened to me.

Me too.

Yup.

It's true.

Baaaa. I don't think so.

4 OUT OF 5 KIDS AGREE

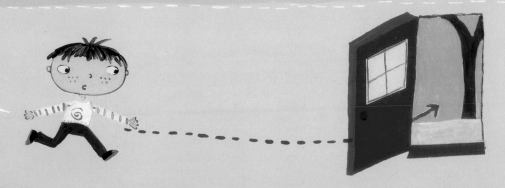

Henry dropped his video game and ran outside.

Inside Henry's body, Henry's heart started beating at 112 beats a minute.

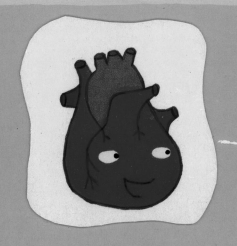

Yay! I'm getting some exercise.

But as soon as Henry got outside,
he stopped running.

Henry's heart wondered why
he was no longer beating very fast.

Sometimes when Henry's heart wants to know
what's going on, he asks the eyes for a report.

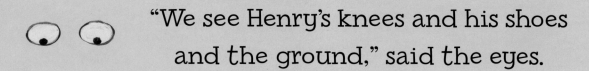
"We see Henry's knees and his shoes and the ground," said the eyes.

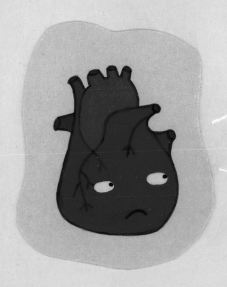

Well, that doesn't sound exciting.

I wonder if his toes are wiggling in his shoes.

Just then, Henry's dad came over and invited Henry to go on a walk.

Let's go, little buddy.

OK, Dad.

Henry and his dad walked

to the center of town.

Henry's heart was very happy.

Wow! I think I got up to 130 beats per minute on that hill.

Then all of a sudden, Henry's heart
started to pump faster and faster.

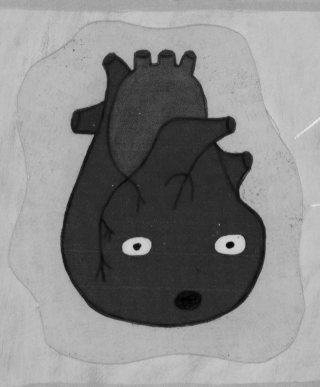

Henry's heart was completely confused.
He shouted to the eyes.

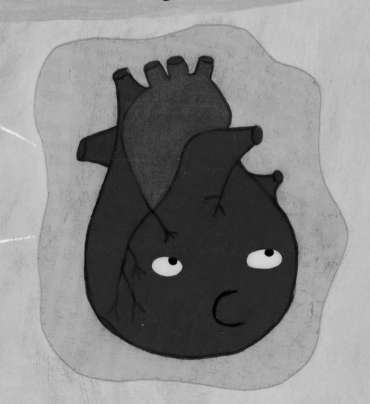

"We see a brown-haired girl in a polka-dotted red dress," reported the eyes.

Henry's heart tried to imagine the girl.

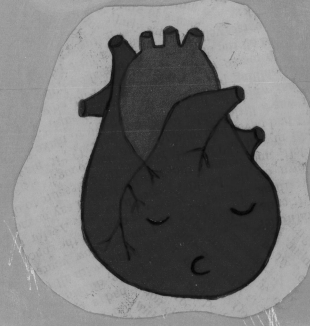

Why am I beating so fast?

THINGS THAT MIGHT MAKE A HEART **BEAT FAST**

	Yes	No		Yes	No
Riding on a roller coaster	X		Meeting someone famous	X	
Eating a pickle		X	Being afraid of someone	X	
Watching a scary movie	X		Seeing an alien	X	
Doing jumping jacks	X		Scraping your knee	X	
Buying toilet paper		X	Falling in love	X	

Henry's heart had two more questions for the eyes.

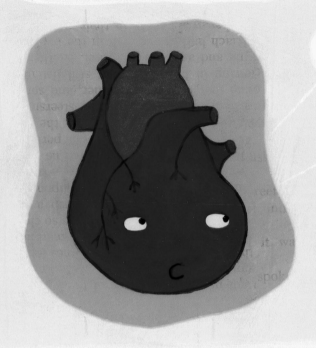

Is the girl scary?

Is the girl famous?

"Not scary, and not famous," answered the eyes. Suddenly Henry's heart knew what was happening.

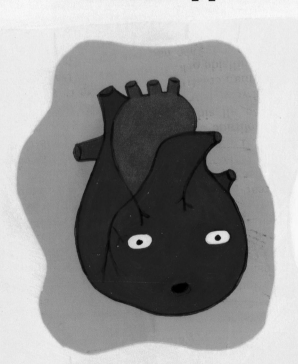

HENRY'S iN LOVE!!!
With the brown-haired girl.

"Wait," said the eyes.
"We have an update.
We see . . .

"That sure is one strange-looking girl," thought Henry's heart.

But Henry's heart was wrong.
Henry wasn't in love with a girl.
He was in love with a puppy.

 **LOVE** is a very powerful feeling.
It can make you feel . . .

STRONG	BRAVE	HOPEFUL
I can do anything.	I shall slay the dragon.	Tomorrow will be a better day.

ENERGETIC	CAREFREE	GENEROUS
I can climb this mountain.	Oh, that's OK.	Would you like my balloon?

PENNY'S PETS

PUPPIES

Dad, can we get her?

Henry's heart has lots of opinions about snacks.

This keeps me healthy! I love them all.

FRESH FRUIT

That's not food!

LOLLIPOP

Finally! A wheel-shaped snack I like.

WHOLE-GRAIN BAGEL

Spoon-licking good.

LOW-FAT YOGURT

A good treat once in a while.

ICE CREAM

One of the natural orange treats.

CARROT STICKS AND LOW-FAT DIP

A great choice on a hot day.

FRUIT POP

Smoothilicious for me. Yummy energy.

LOW-FAT SMOOTHIE

OK if it's not covered with salt and butter.

POPCORN

A dangerous wheel of fat and sugar.

DONUT WITH SPRINKLES

Tasty!

DRIED FRUIT AND NUTS

Once in a while it's nice to eat a lion.

ANIMAL CRACKERS

Crunchy, salty disks of doom.

POTATO CHIPS

It's easy to eat these on the go, and they make me feel strong.

LOW-FAT CHEESE STICKS

Sometimes losing love can affect the stomach.

I'm not hungry, Dad.

Well, that's unusual.

When Henry and his dad got home, Henry went to his room to lie on his bed and stare at the ceiling.

This was not normal Henry behavior.

Henry's heart was concerned. He asked the eyes for an update every fifteen minutes.

Now what do you see?

Every time the answer was the same.

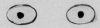

"Nothing much," said the eyes, "just the ceiling in a color somewhere between

and

MILK WHITE

BUTTER YELLOW."

Or mashed-up turnip white?

Well, that's disgusting.

Are you sure it's not more like corncob yellow?

Ugh! These are cold.

After several days of unusual Henry behavior, Henry's family and friends started to worry.

Henry's heart was worried too.

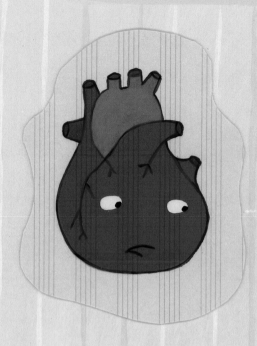

I feel sluggish and tired. I haven't had any exercise in days.

Finally, Henry's mother decided she had to take Henry to the doctor.

Don't worry, Henry. I'm sure Dr. Terry will be able to help you.

Dr. Terry examined Henry. He checked

his eyes, ✓

his nose, ✓

his mouth, ✓

and his ears. ✓

He listened carefully to Henry's heart. After all that, he and Henry had a nice, long chat.

Here is your prescription. This will make Henry feel better.

Thank you, Doctor.

EYE CHART
DXURP
NCANV
OJSBLCT
TXHEALTHBU
OARDEFXMP

On the way home, Henry's mother drove right past the pharmacy. She didn't stop to drop off the prescription.

When Henry's dad arrived, there was all sorts of noise in the kitchen. This made Henry a little curious.

He was even more curious when his sister ran into his room and yelled . . .

MOM SAYS YOU HAVE TO COME DOWNSTAIRS TO THE KITCHEN RIGHT NOW TO TAKE YOUR MEDICINE!

Henry got up and slowly walked toward the kitchen, then all of a sudden his heart was racing.

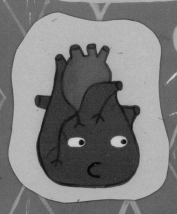

Whoa!

What's going on?

Why am I beating so fast?

IT WAS LOVE!

Henry's heart was very excited about the new medicine.

I feel so strong and healthy.

Every day there was . . .

walking,

chasing,

running,

and playing.

Henry's heart loved all of it.

But most of all he loved nighttime
when he could hear the soft beat of
another heart right beside him.